Stinky Boys Club

Enough Is ENOUGH!

By Jodi Carse and Maria Gallagher

Illustrated by Brie Spangler

Grosset & Dunlap ◉ New York

The Same...

Sam and MJ are twins.

Red hair

Freckles

Older by one minute

Sam

Sam and MJ's parents think that boys and girls should be raised exactly the same. And Mom's got the pictures to prove it!

Sam and MJ, Age 1—Sam loves his strained peas!

Halloween, Age 4—The cutest little firefighters ever!

Christmas, Age 5—The kids love their new trucks.

Tap Class, Age 7—Mrs. Patty Buree's tap class—so much fun!

Of course, they aren't EXACTLY the same . . .

MJ is better at SPORTS than Sam.

Big deal!

MJ is also NEATER than Sam.

And she never gets in TROUBLE for making food come out of her nose.

Of course, there are some things Sam does better than MJ. He has the best collection of stupid jokes—2,674 and counting.

Sam is also the best at annoying people.

Sometimes he will go all day speaking only in a ROBOT voice.

Or he'll SHOUT random numbers when someone is trying to count.

Or he'll HUM the Batman theme song over and over and over . . .

But the one thing Sam does better than anyone is come up with pranks. Not just everyday, ordinary, average pranks—Sam is a planner, an inventor, a leader of men. Well, he's the leader of the Only Boys Club.

The Only Boys Club is the one place that MJ is not allowed. Even Sam's mom has to admit that ONLY boys means NO girls. At the Only Boys Club, Sam can be as annoying as he wants to be—and best of all, he can come up with all kinds of pranks. The Only Boys Club pranks are

the biggest, the slimiest, the silliest . . . and the STINKIEST!

One time they trained the mean neighbor's dog to **POOP** right on his own front step.

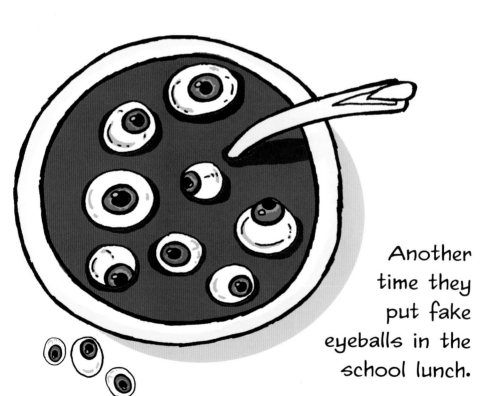

Another time they put fake eyeballs in the school lunch.

Then there was the time they clipped all the hedges in the neighborhood to look like space aliens.

Or when . . . well, there are a lot of stories, but this is the story of how the Only Boys Club became the

Our story starts on the first day of third grade.

Sam tried to picture The Rock or
Stone Cold Steve Austin at a dance
class . . .

but he couldn't.

Sam had managed to keep his friends from finding out about tap class by saying he had lots of chores to do. But now MJ was going to blow his cover!

It couldn't get worse!

"I've got more!" Sam said, still laughing. "A whole new list I made up last night!"

Great Jokes

#2765
What do you call a lazy baby kangaroo?
– A POUCH potato!

#2766
What is the funniest key in the world?
– A Monkey!

#2767
Knock, Knock!
– Who's there?
Boo.
– Boo Who?
Don't cry! It's only a joke!

MJ rolled her eyes. "Well, if <u>you</u> had been listening, <u>you</u> would have just heard that our tap class is performing at the fall talent show next week!"

"Urgh!" Sam cried, making the noise he always made when something really awful happened. "What worse could happen?"

"Everyone will see you dancing with Pru," MJ said. "That'll be worse."

Sam sunk down in his seat. "Thanks for reminding me," he said. "Pru! Urgh!"

A Word About Pru

Pru is perfect. Always.

Perfect hair

Perfect teeth

Perfect clothes

Perfectly perfect everything

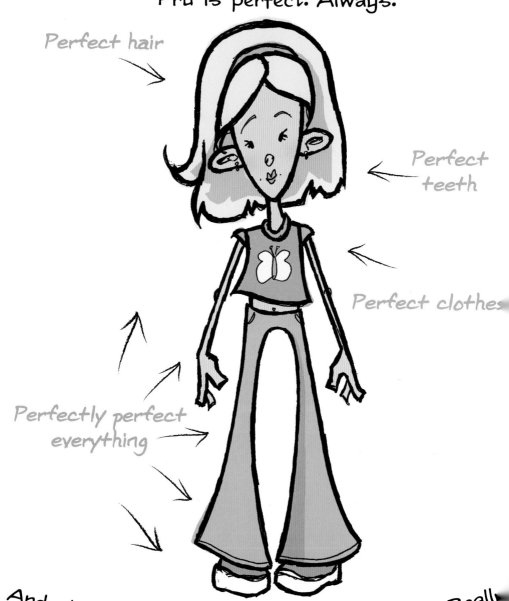

And she is the girliest girl who ever lived. Really!

And to be seen with Pru! Tap dancing! In front of the whole school!

"Urgh!" Sam moaned again. "I've got to get out of this!"

Sam realized there was only one thing to do: call an emergency meeting of the Only Boys Club.

Meet the Boys!

Alex

Zip

Monster

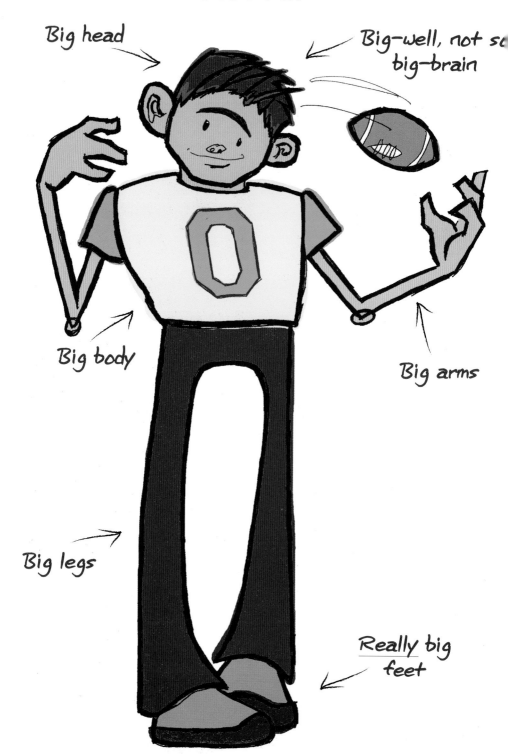

Gus

At recess, the boys met up at their usual spot by the swings. "Men," Sam began, "we have a serious problem. And it involves tap dancing."

"Tap dancing? What's that?" Monster asked.

"You know—tap dancing," Alex said. "Like this." He showed off a few steps.

Sam took a deep breath. "Anyway, listen up. My mom made me take tap classes this summer. And now I have to dance in the talent show."

"Oh, no!" Gus cried.

"I know, it's terrible," Sam sighed.

"Not 'oh, no' that," Gus said. "'Oh, no,' my scab fell off and I can't find it."

"Okay—Operation Find Gus's Scab! Move out!" Sam commanded. The boys spread across the playground, looking under every swing, rock, and chewed-up piece of gum for Gus's scab.

Zip found it in two seconds. "HereitisGus!"

"Thanks—it's a really good one," Gus said.

"Back to business," said Sam. "This is bad. Probably the worst thing that could happen."

"Don't say that! Whenever you say that, something even worse happens," Gus said.

"Yup," Monster said. "Like here come MJ, Pru, and Missy . . ."

A Word on Missy

Missy is the smartest girl in the entire school.

$E=MC^2$

$\sqrt{99}$

First to be EVERY teacher's pet

First to raise hand

First to finis test

First to spell antidisestablishmentarianism

Pru walked right up to Sam and batted her eyelashes. "Hi, Sam . . ." she cooed.

Missy, of course, began talking right away. "Hi, guys, what's going on over here? Are you planning something? What are you doing for the science project? I have this great idea for an array-electrometer exhibit with a visible panel that lets you experience an electromagnetic field. I call it an 'e-panel.' How it works is . . ."

Sam rolled his eyes. "Guys, we need someplace we can talk

PRIVATELY!"

The Super-Top-Secret-No-Girls-Allowed-At-All Clubhouse

Sam had another brilliant idea. He realized that what the Only Boys Club needed was a boys-only clubhouse. And this was not going to be just your ordinary top-secret clubhouse. It would be the world's first super-top-secret-no-girls-allowed-at-all clubhouse with state-of-the-art technology . . . well, at least the best technology they could make out of old video cameras and vacuum cleaner parts.

The girls were *very* curious about what the boys were up to.

Does Mom know you have her old computer?

Like one bee said to the other . . . MIND YOUR OWN BZZZZZZNESS!

So the boys worked day and night
(well, at least until bedtime) until finally,
their clubhouse was done.

Suddenly, there was an angry knock on the door. It was MJ, Pru, and Missy—and they meant business.

Missy handed Sam a notice. "This is to inform you that we've filed a petition with the school and the neighborhood association. The Only Boys Club is discriminatory toward girls and is therefore ILLEGAL."

"What does that mean?" Monster wondered.

"It means you're going to have to let us join, or we'll take this all the way to the Supreme Court!" And with that, the girls turned on their heels and left.

Sam banged his fist into his hand. "Men, are we going to stand for this?"

"Stand?" asked Monster. "But we're sitting."

So Sam turned to Joe Comp. "Joe, how can we keep the girls from joining our club?" he asked.

Joe bleeped and blipped for a moment, then answered, "The question is—why do they want to join?"

"Because they know that we're the best and they want to learn our secrets!" Sam replied.

"So why not show them your secrets," Joe laughed.

"WHAT???? No way!" yelled all the boys—all except Sam.

"Hmmm," he said. "I think I see what you're getting at."

Join the Club

The bathroom Sam picked for the special meeting had been closed ever since anyone could remember—and it hadn't been cleaned in just as long. It was slimy and moldy and mildewy and green. In a word, perfect.

"Right this way, ladies. Sorry about the mess," Alex said politely, holding open the door.

Pru held her nose. "Hi, Sam," she said in a high voice.

Sam held open his arms. "Welcome to the ONLY Boys Club. Which you might have noticed is held in the boys bathroom, so that usually means NO GIRLS, but . . ."

"Yeah, yeah," MJ interrupted. "Get on with it."

Sam glared at her. "Well, since you were soooooooo curious to see what goes on . . . Monster, why don't you start?"

"Today's meeting is a cooking class," Monster announced.

"Ohhhh," squealed Pru. "I love cooking. Sam, will you be my partner?"

"We're going to make throw-up," Monster added.

"I think I'm gonna be sick," said Pru, making a face.

Recipe for Throw-up

1. First take some chewed-up corn chips

2. Next add some orange juice

3. Oatmeal with green food coloring adds texture

4. Then mix in strawberry milk shake to taste

5. And finish with a can of creamed corn

The girls were too grossed-out to care about joining the Only Boys Club anymore! But there was still the problem of the talent show, and Sam's brain had been working overtime.

"I know Joe thinks I should pretend to be sick. But my mother will never believe me," Sam sighed.

"True," his friends agreed.

"Besides, that wouldn't be as much fun," Sam laughed. "If the girls don't show up, they'll have to call off the whole show!"

"Why wouldn't the girls show up?" Monster asked.

"Oh, I'm sure we can find a way to make them stay home!" Sam exclaimed.

The morning of the talent show, Zip snuck into class before everyone else and sprinkled itching powder on the erasers.

Don't you think itching powder looks just like chalk?

Not long after Zip slipped out of class, Missy got to school. As the official teacher's pet, she just loved to clean the blackboard and beat the erasers.

By the time Miss Apple started class, Missy was feeling . . . itchy.

"So, who can tell me . . ." Miss Apple began.

Missy's hand shot up in the air.

"Missy, I haven't even finished the question!" Miss Apple said.

"Sorry. It was just an itch," Missy said.

"All right," Miss Apple started again. "So who can tell me the . . . Missy, are you paying attention?"

Missy was trying so hard to scratch her back that she hardly heard what the teacher said.

"Huh? I'm sorry, what?" Missy asked.

Some of the kids started laughing.

"This is very unlike you, Missy," Miss Apple said with a frown. "One more disruption and I'll have to send you to the principal's office."

"I'm sorry," Missy repeated miserably.

Now, the only time Missy had ever been to the principal's office was to accept an award.

So she tried her hardest to pay attention and not to **ITCH!**

When she couldn't stand it any longer, she broke down in an all-out itching frenzy. She was crazy itchy!

"Missy!" Miss Apple scolded her, pointing toward the door. Missy got up and began the long, lonely walk to the principal's office— *itching* all the way.

By that afternoon, MJ was suspicious. Someone had glued the armholes of her costume together. She called Missy and Pru.

"Girls, we have a problem," MJ began.

"Oh, MJ, I don't think I can do the show!" Missy interrupted. "I've come down with a mysterious rash. I think it might be Itchthyosis."

"I don't think I can be in the show either," Pru moaned. "My hair, my face! Someone put baby oil in my shampoo and switched my soap. Now my hair is greasy and my skin is splotchy! I can't be seen in public like this."

Hmmm, MJ thought. My costume ruined, Missy's mysterious rash, Pru's oily shampoo . . . I think someone is trying to stop the show . . . and I think I know just who it is.

"Pull yourself together, girls," she said. "I have a plan. The show MUST go on . . . and it will!"

The Show Must NOT Go On

Sam and the boys thought that their plan to cancel the show was foolproof. So imagine their surprise when they heard that the show was still on! This called for drastic measures.

"Men, this calls for drastic measures," Sam said.

Monster gasped. "You don't mean . . ."

"That's right," Sam said. "It's time for the ultimate work of fart."

Anyone can make a fart, but to make a **really good, really loud, really stinky one,** well, now, that's a science. After months of experimenting, the boys had found just the right recipe for their masterpiece, the

DIAL-A-FART MACHINE.

3 dirty diapers (borrowed from Zip's little brother)

1 dozen rotten eggs

1 bag garbage

1 set unwashed gym clothes

and finally

10 dirty boy's socks worn for a week

Places, Everyone!

The big show was about to begin. The girls were ready . . . and so were the boys. (Well, almost.)

Missy was first to go onstage. She tried to leap gracefully, but a long, high-pitched sound came from under her skirt.

MJ was next . . . but her dip sounded like she stepped on a duck.

Finally, it was Pru's turn. The boys turned the dial to Silent-But-DEADLY. At first nothing happened, but as she went into her final twirl across the stage, a trail of stinky green gas followed behind her.

"Now for the grand finale!" Sam yelled, turning the dial to EXPLOSION.

The Girls Strike Back

The boys were celebrating their victory when Mrs. Buree and the girls stormed up to them. Imagine you've just stolen all the honey from a group of hungry bears or taken a bone from a rabid dog or stepped on the tail of a Tasmanian devil . . . you are still not even close to imagining how mad a group of humiliated tap dancing girls can get.

It's too **awful** to show you what happened . . .

But the next day at school, MJ came prepared.

Introducing The Stinky Boys Club

"This is terrible!" Sam moaned. "The entire school is laughing at us! Our reputation is ruined!"

"I never had a reputation to begin with," replied Gus.

"Everyone is too scared of me to laugh in my face," Monster said.

"Ijustwannarunaway," said Zip.

Alex shrugged. "Come on, guys, it wasn't that bad. At least it's over now."

Sam stood up. "You know what I think?" he said. "The best thing to do is pretend that we meant to do that. And get back at those girls! If they want stinky, they'll get stinky . . ."

"Let's make a pact," Sam continued. "From now on, we hereby swear to stop at nothing to get even with the girls. Let no chair go without a whoopee cushion . . .

no shoelaces go untied together . . .

no shirt unstained with magic ink.

We will use every dirty trick, every gross-out gag, and every sneaky, slimy, stinky practical joke!"

And that's how the Stinky Boys Club started. And what are the girls going to do about it? Well, that's another story.